Benson and Cookie the Care Home Cat

by Susan Dodd

Illustrated by Abbie Bryson

Grosvenor House
Publishing Limited

The right of Susan Dodd to be identified as the author of this
work has been asserted by him in accordance with Section 78
of the Copyright, Designs and Patents Act 1988

The book cover picture is copyright to Susan Dodd

This book is published by
Grosvenor House Publishing Ltd
Link House
140 The Broadway, Tolworth, Surrey, KT6 7HT.
www.grosvenorhousepublishing.co.uk

This book is a work of fiction. Any resemblance to
people or events, past or present, is purely coincidental.

A CIP record for this book
is available from the British Library

ISBN 978-1-83975-941-3

For all at Fir Close Care Centre

Benson the Cat lived in the old workshop
With Mr Elvic, who worked non-stop.
He taps and tinkers with wonky machines,
As Benson watches whilst eating sardines.

Cookie the Cat lived at Woodlands Care Home,
With people who couldn't walk on their own.
Benson and Cookie were the best of friends,
Meeting up at the home on most weekends.

Sunning themselves by the fast-running stream
As Mr Elvic pushed his mowing machine.
"Do you like living here, Cookie, my mate?"
"Benson, my friend, it is purrfectly great."

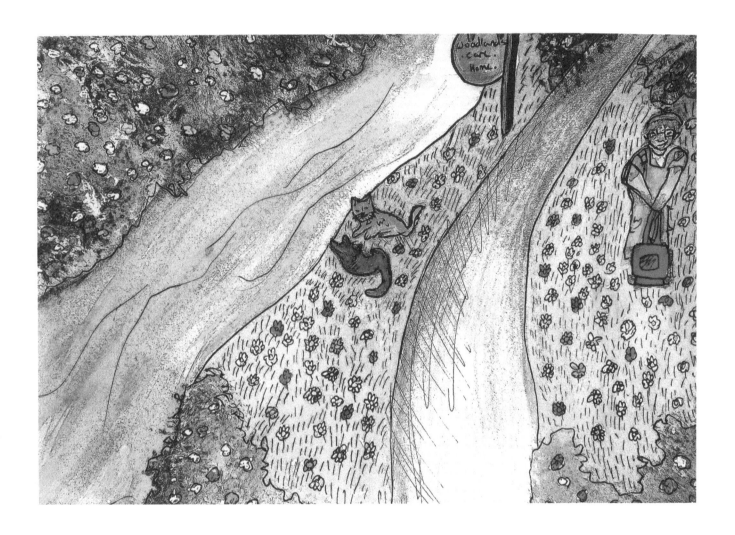

7

Ivy was having a snooze in her chair,
Snoring loudly, and dreaming of elsewhere.
Soon, Dowter the dog came into the room,
Wagging his tail like a big, fluffy broom.

Dowter put a big, black paw on Ivy's knee,
And she opened her eyes and smiled with glee.
"We are so lucky to know such caring folk,"
Said Cookie, as Ivy gave Dowter a stroke.

Dowter was a playful dog, never sitting still.
Seeing a ball of wool, he thought, *"This is brill"*.
He grabbed one end and ran round and round,
Covering poor Ivy 'til she couldn't be found.

The elderly people laughed out loud
As Dowter played on, looking so proud.
Anna arrived with some cakes on a tray,
And soon the lounge was in disarray.

Tripping over Dowter as
she came through the door,
Anna and the cakes landed all over the floor.
Dowter licked his lips, thinking this was his tea,
Eating two cakes before making it three.

Benson walked past the church
with its very tall spire,
Hoping it's fish for tea, from the deep fat fryer.
Wiggling his whiskers as he squeezed
through the cat flap,
Benson sniffed the fish smell and
ate up every last scrap.

Benson snuggled down in his bed
by the warm stove.
Mouse peeped out, and a spider
swung down from the web he wove.
Benson dreamed of the happy life he was living,
Lucky to have friends so caring and giving.

Sitting in the lounge, they waited
for Mrs Gee to sing.
"She is very kind," said Cookie,
"but makes such a din."
Hands covered ears to block out the loud racket,
And Alison covered her head with her red jacket.

"Later on," said Cookie,
"we have a treat to come,
It's Albert's birthday,
so no-one should look glum.
There are balloons, and
Cook has made a special cake,
So don't eat too much and get a tummy ache."

Great fun was had playing every game.
To enjoy the party was their main aim.
Albert enjoyed having everyone there,
As they all brought gifts to show that they care.

As everyone wished each other goodnight,
Benson and Cookie sat in the moonlight.
Benson said, "I know why you like living here,
It's a loving, caring, happy atmosphere."

"Thank you, Mr Elvic," said Benson quietly,
"For helping me live my life so happily."
"Why, Benson, it is because we are a great team."
Soon Benson was dreaming
the dreams that only cats can dream.

About the Author

Susan was born in Louth, Lincolnshire and was educated in the local schools. Susan's English teacher once said to her, "Susan, if you don't write a book one day I shall eat my hat." She never forgot those words and went on to have three books published about Benson, a talking cat. The books are set on Cinder Lane in Louth, in her father's workshop.

Susan lives in the nearby village of Fotherby with her husband Richard, and with the rest of the family are avid Grimsby Town football fans.

Benson and Cookie the Care Home Cat is the first picture book Susan has produced in response to the plentiful requests from so many parents.

About the Illustrator

Abbie Bryson shared a passion for art from an early age and would fill countless sketchbooks with doodles and portraits. When aged just 14, she was presented with the opportunity to illustrate this book and was "over the moon".

Abbie hopes to carry this passion into her adult life to make it her full-time career.

Lightning Source UK Ltd.
Milton Keynes UK
UKHW020628290322
400761UK00005B/51